20KM/H

WOSHIBAI

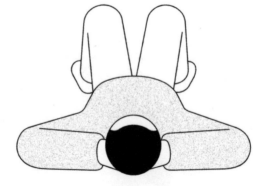

我是白・WOSHIBAI

我是白是生活在上海的插畫師和漫畫家。大部分作品是單色的，極簡而專注，在單幀和多幀之間跳躍，能夠以令人印象深刻的輕鬆構建敘事。曾為《紐約客》、《彭博商業周刊》、蘋果 Apple 和 Chanel 等知名媒體或品牌繪製作品。

2017 年開始創作漫畫，並通過社交媒體發佈，目前已出版漫畫作品集：《遊戲》（中國）、《20KM/H》（比利時）。

● Instagram: @woshibaii　　● Twitter: @woshibai

20KM/H

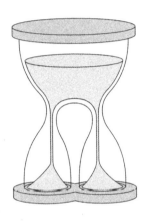

bridge

橋

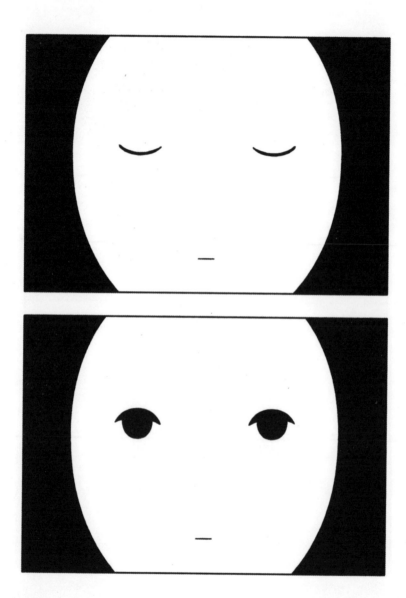

bridge

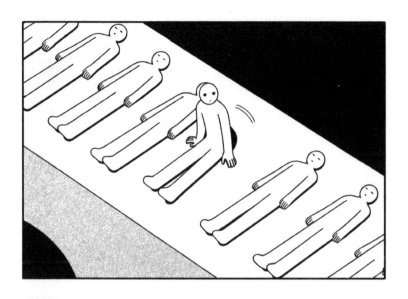

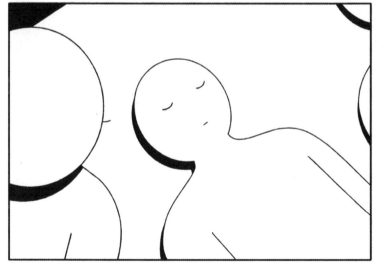

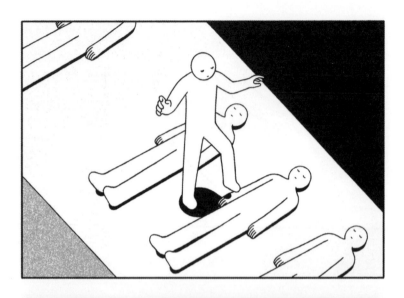

bridge

橋

bridge

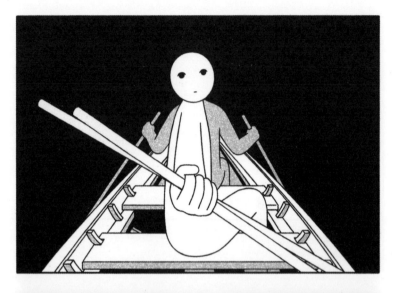

bridge

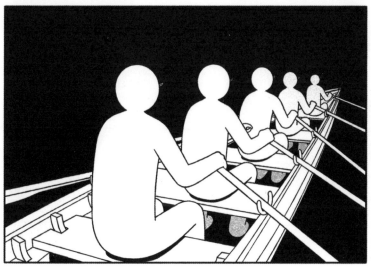

bridge

bottle

阿 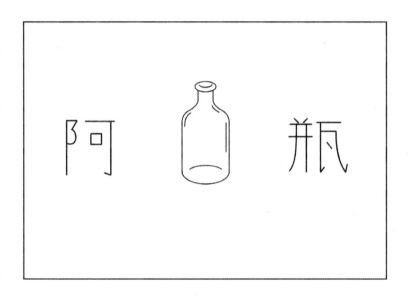 瓶

bottle

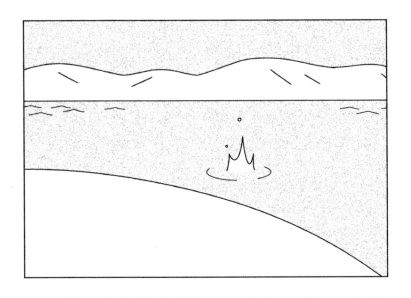

阿瓶

bottle

阿瓶

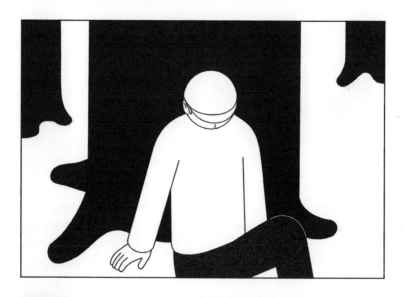

bottle

storm

storm

storm

暴風雨

storm

storm

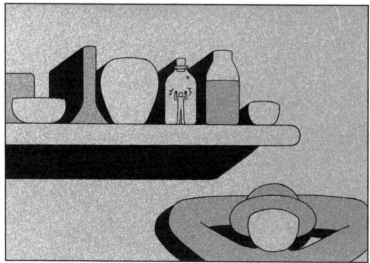

暴風雨

storm

news

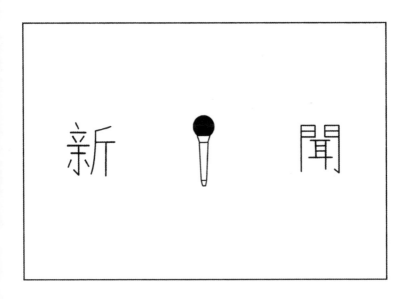

新 聞

news

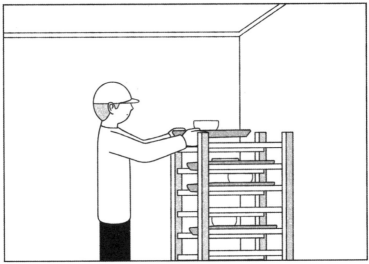

news

news

beach

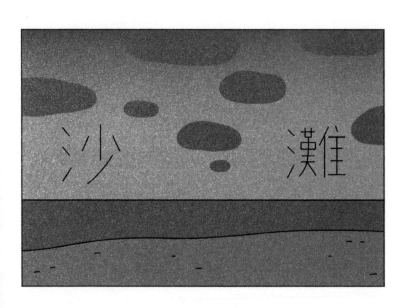

沙漠

beach

沙灘

beach

moon

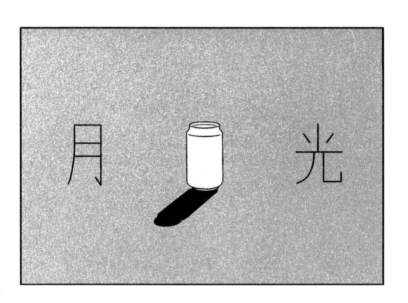

月　光

moon

moon

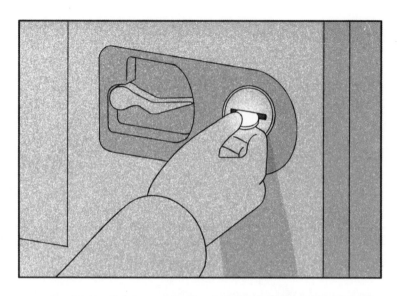

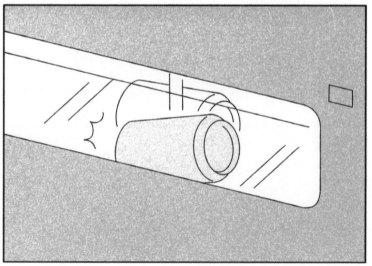

moon

sweep

掃　　除

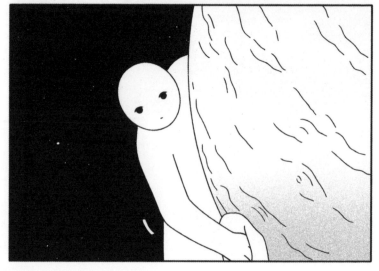

sweep

掃除

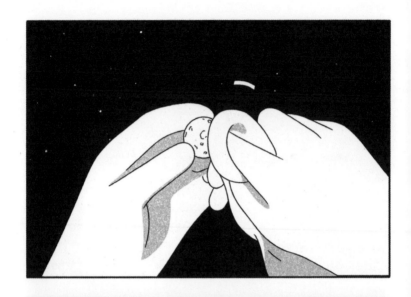

sweep

掃除

sweep

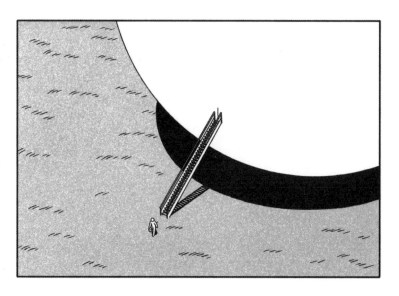

sweep

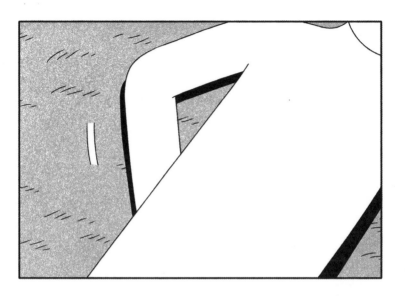

掃除

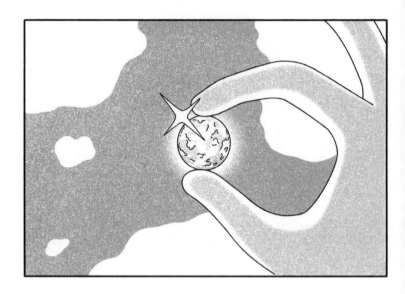

sweep

gift

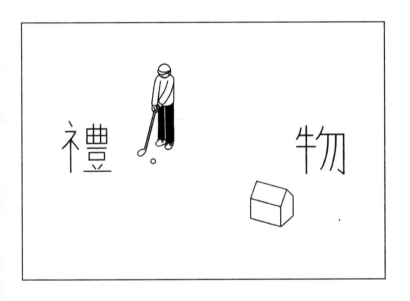

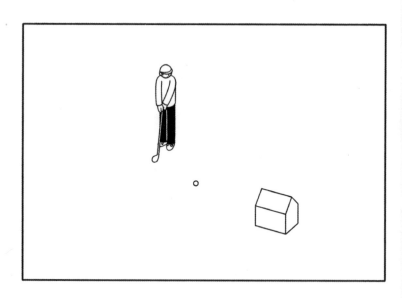

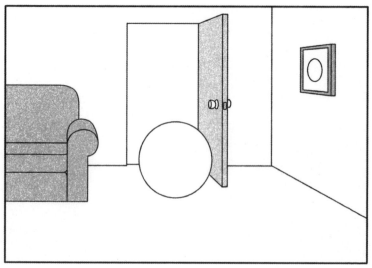

gift

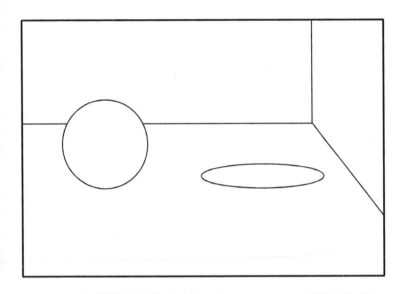

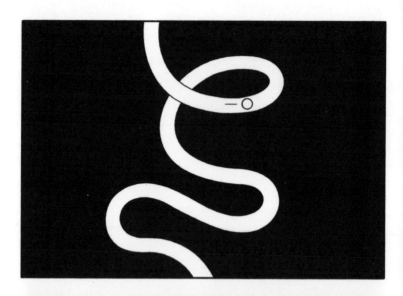

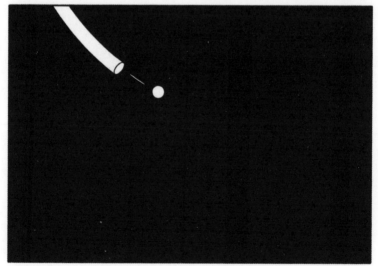

gift

gift

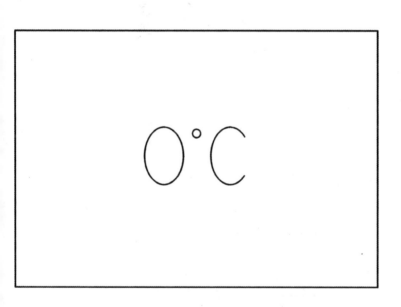

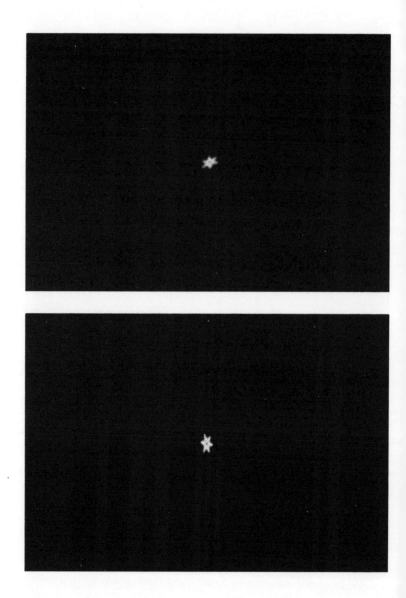

0°C

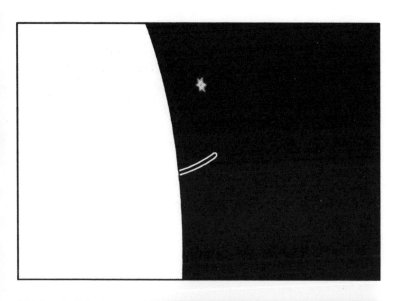

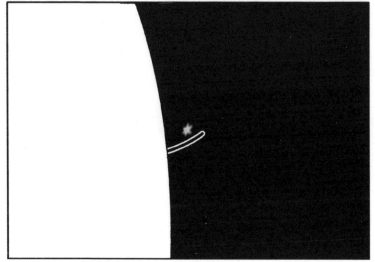

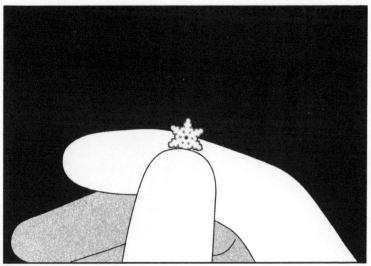

0°C

string

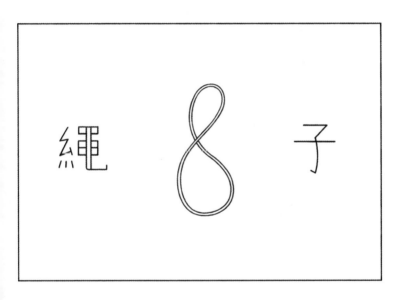

縄 8 子

string

string

繩子

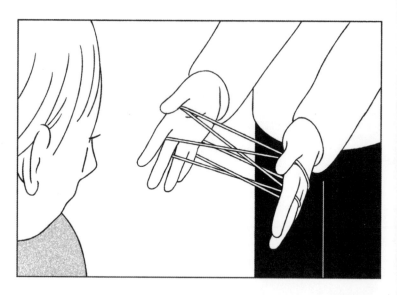

string

collect

収集

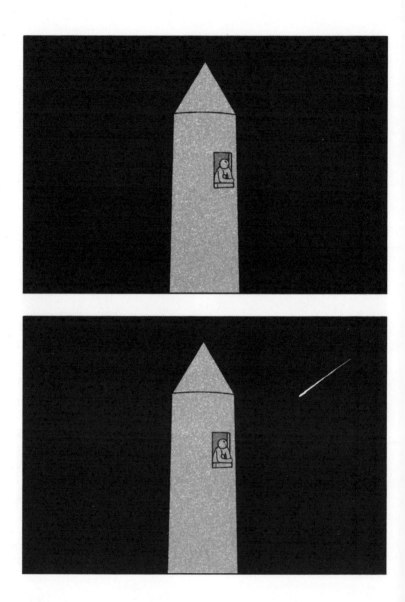

collect

收集

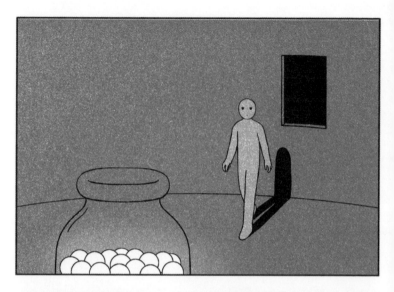

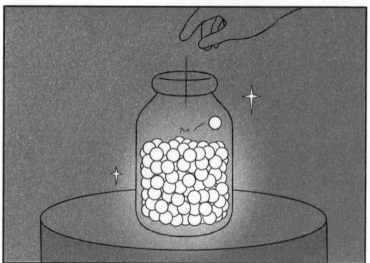

collect

record

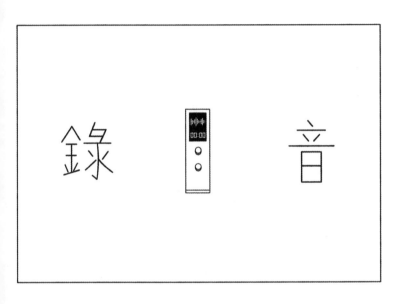

録　音

record

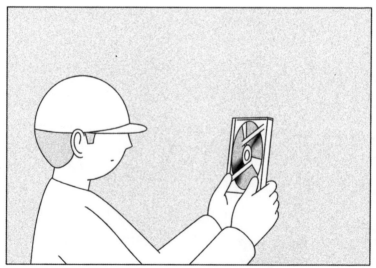

record

錄音

island

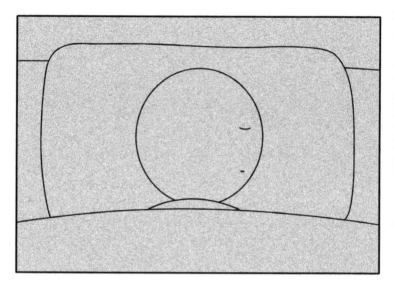

island

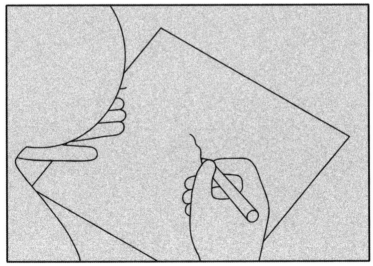

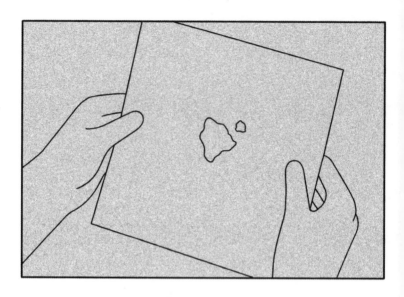

island

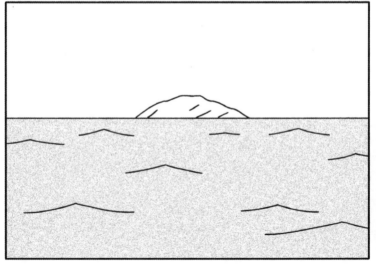

island

ruler

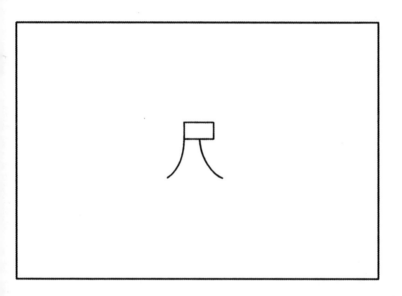

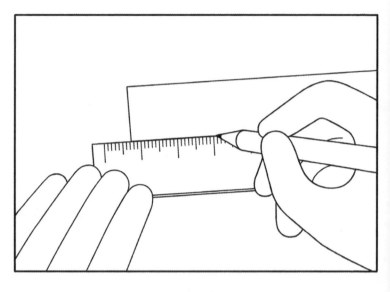

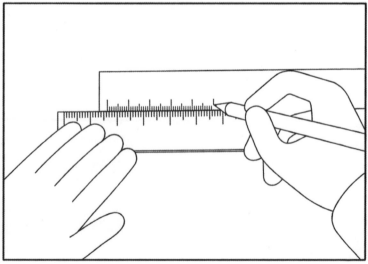

ruler

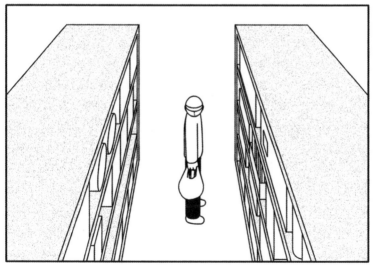

ruler

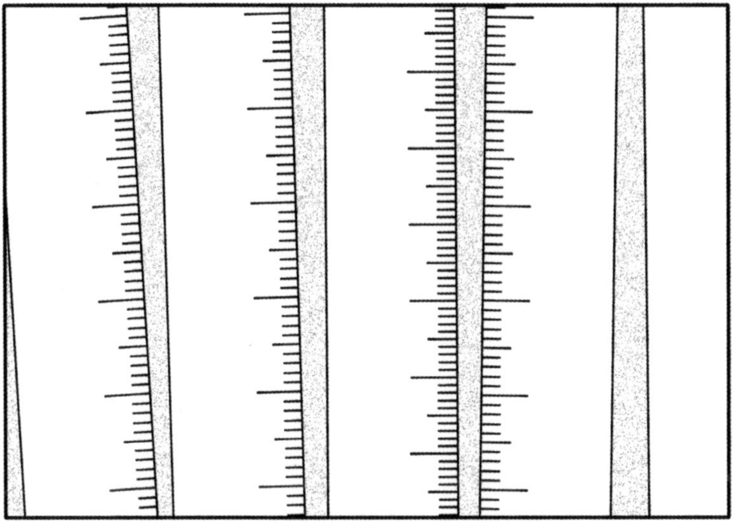

afternoon

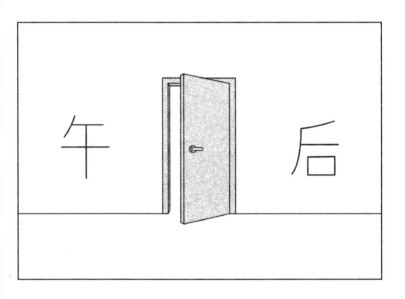

午 后

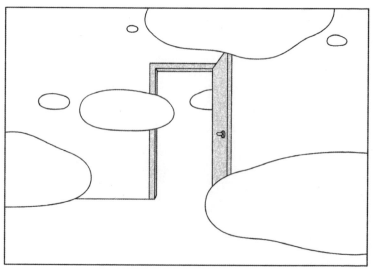

afternoon

午后

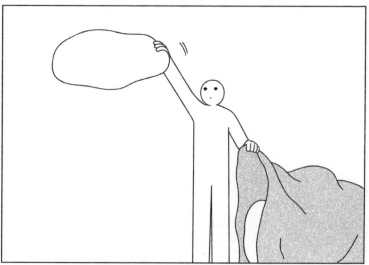

afternoon

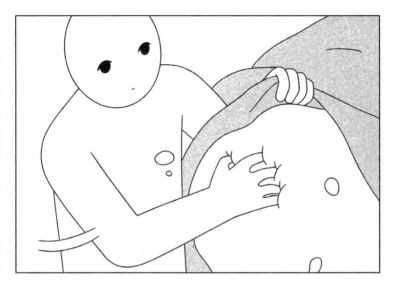

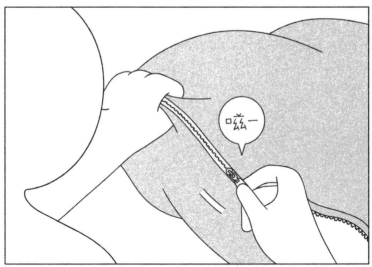

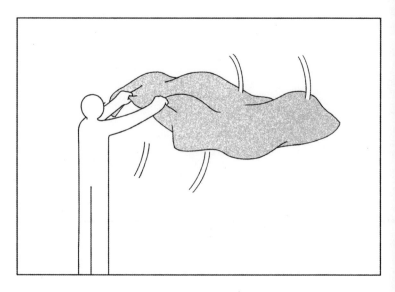

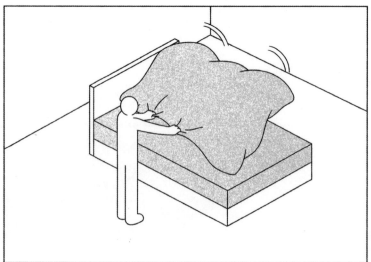

afternoon

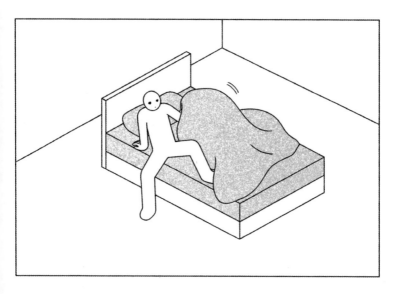

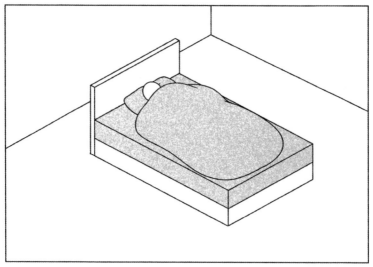

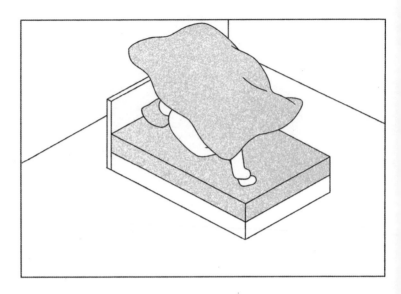

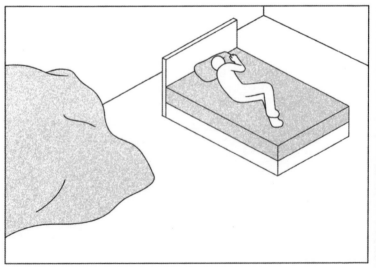

afternoon

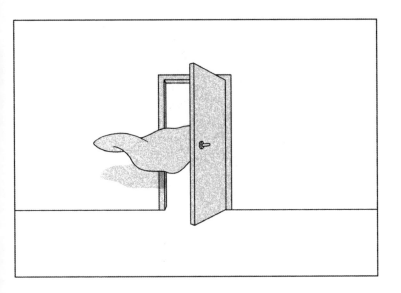

午后

thief

小 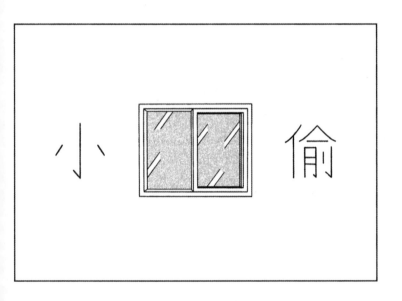 偷

thief

小偷

thief

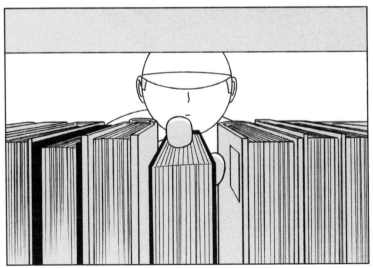

小偷

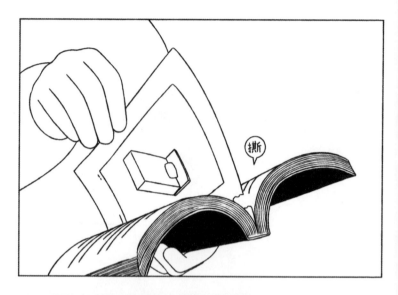

thief

小偷

thief

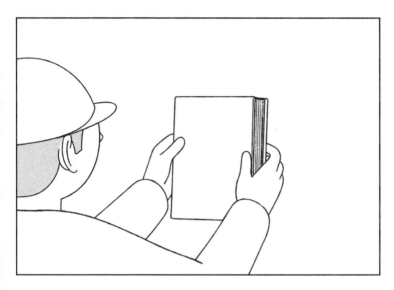

thief

carve

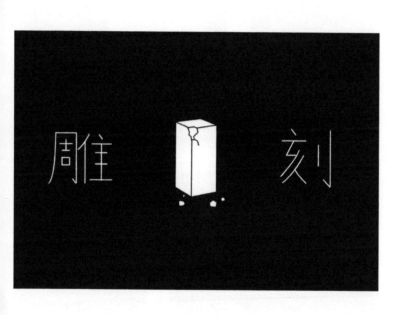

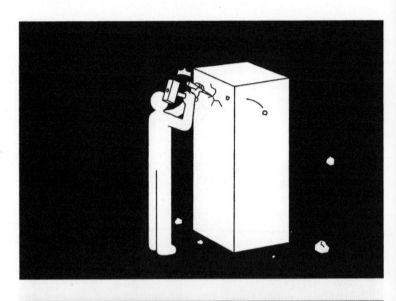

carve

雕刻

carve

雕刻

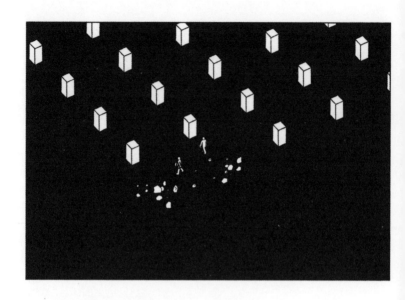

carve

walk

散 歩

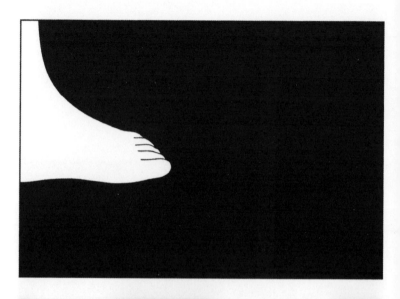

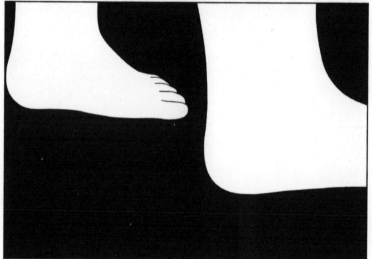

walk

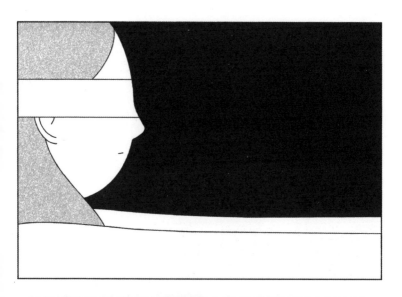

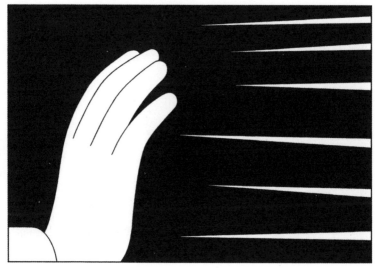

散歩

walk

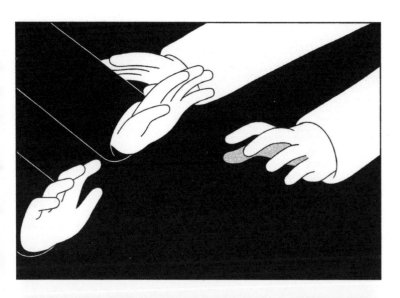

walk

walk

cobble

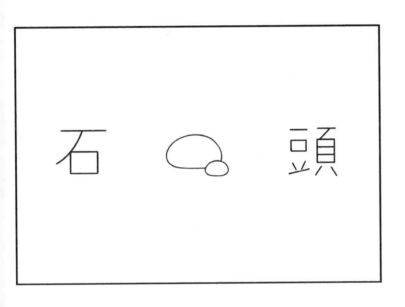

石 〇 頭

cobble

石頭

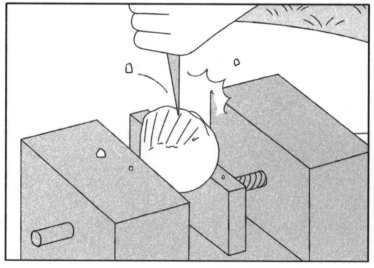

cobble

石頭

cobble

石頭

domino

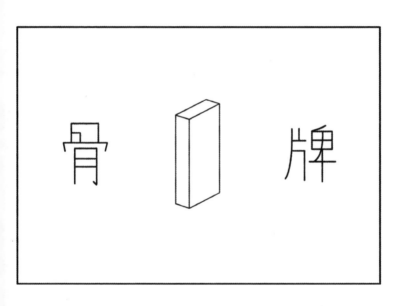

骨　牌

domino

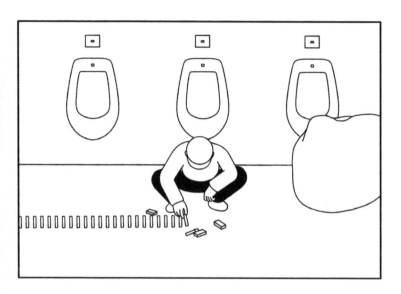

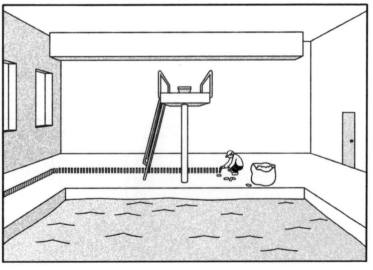

domino

domino

direction

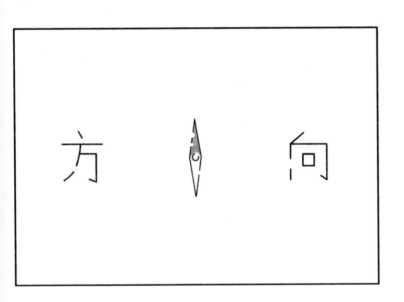

方　　　向

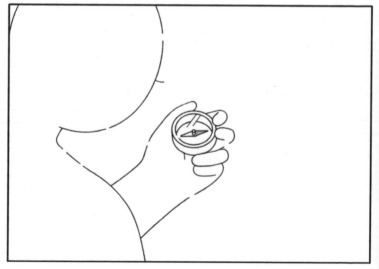

direction

direction

lost

失 物

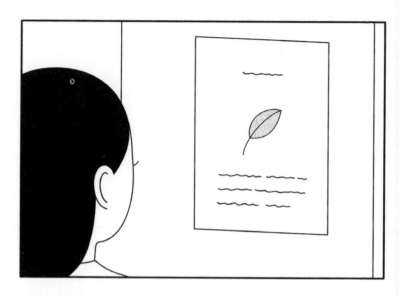

lost

失物

lost

lost

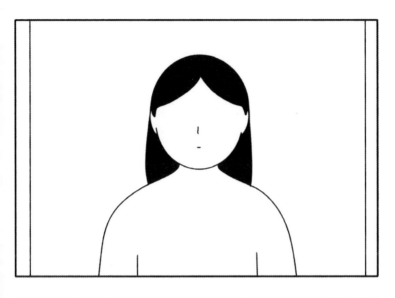

失物

pupa

pupa

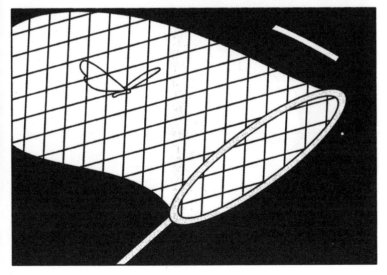

蛹

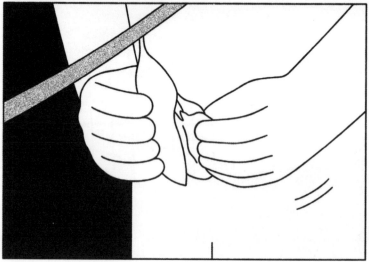

pupa

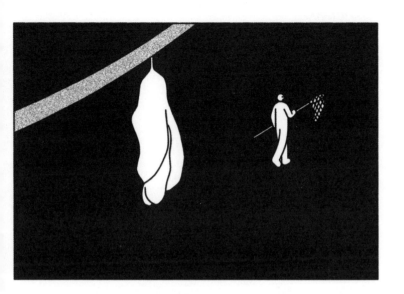

蛹

danger

危 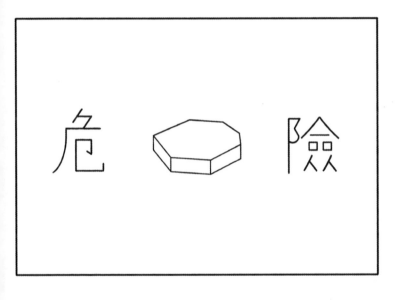 險

danger

danger

ice

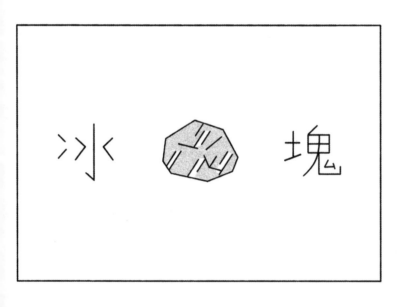

ice

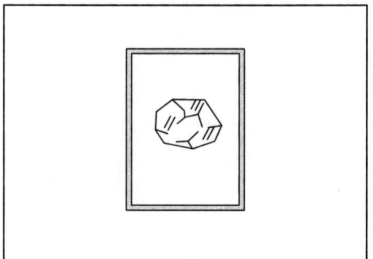

ice

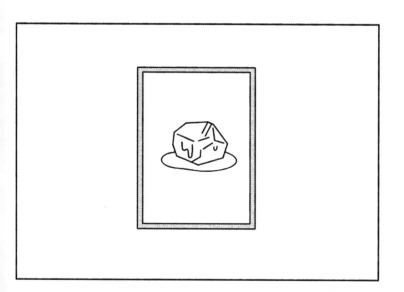

冰塊

winter

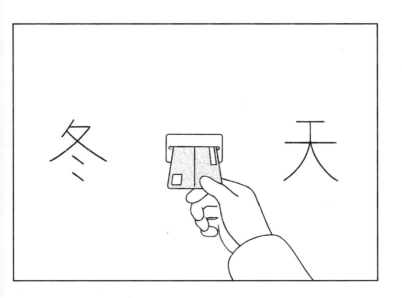

冬　天

winter

winter

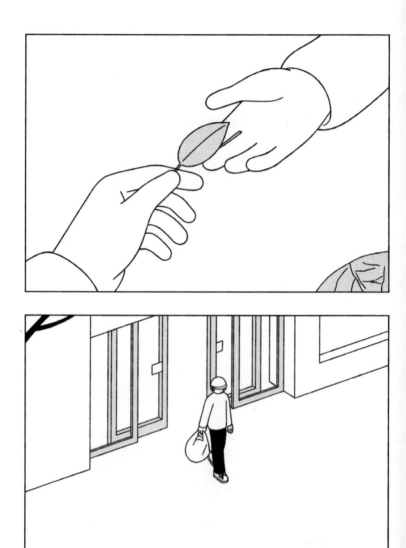

winter

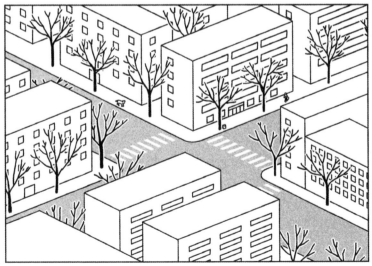

illustration

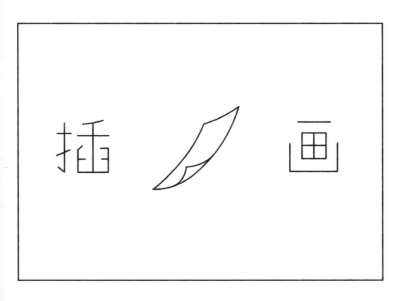

插 ╱ 画

illustration

illustration

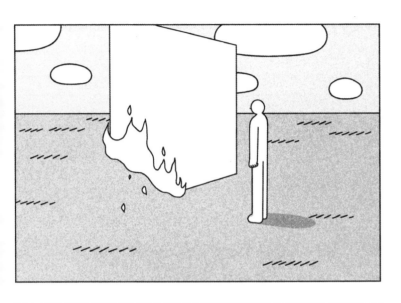

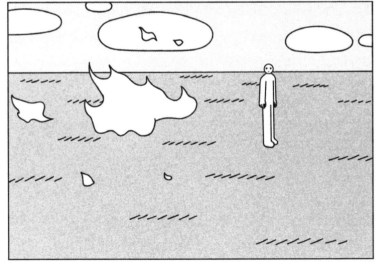

illustration

chair

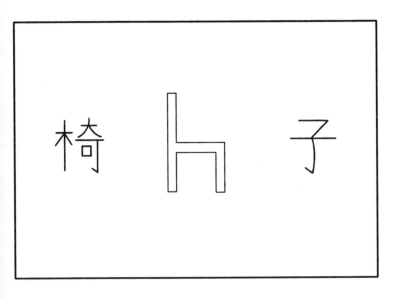

椅　ㄏ　子

chair

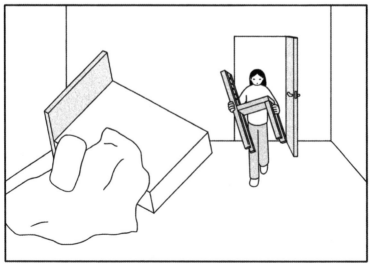

椅子

chair

椅子

clean

打 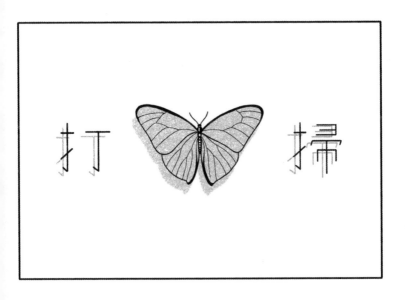 掃

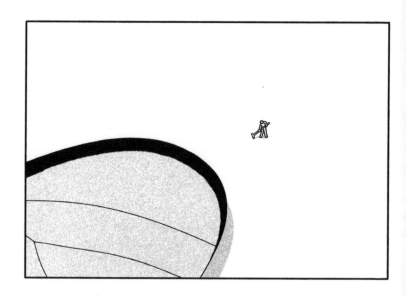

clean

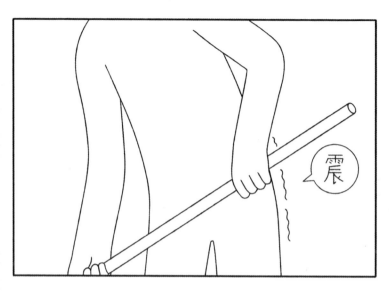

打掃

clean

打掃

clean

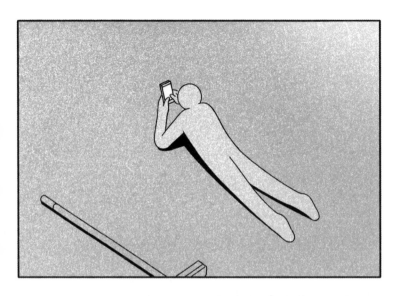

打掃

clean

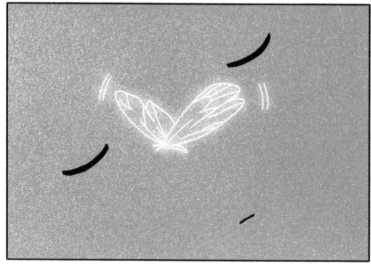

打掃

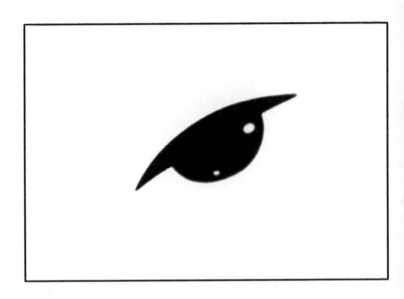

clean

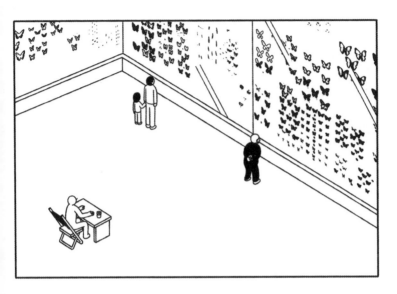

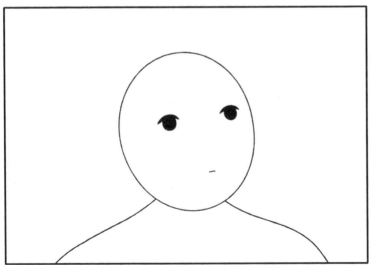

打掃

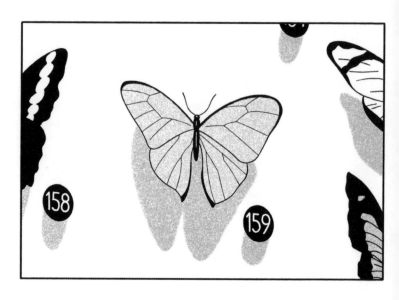

doorman

警言 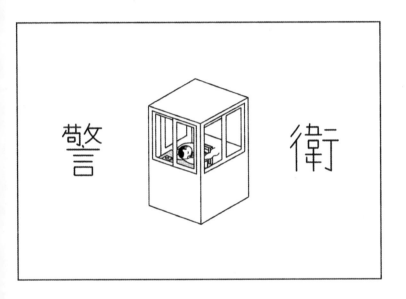 衛

doorman

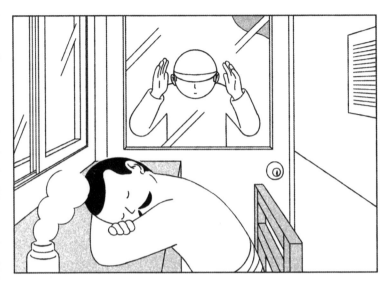

警衛

doorman

警衛

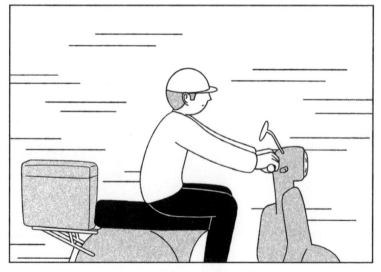

doorman

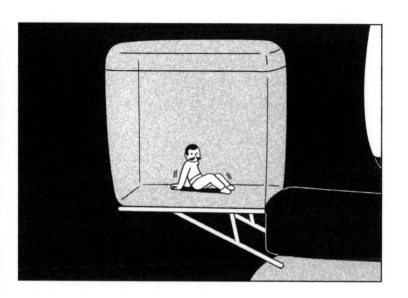

fiction

小　說

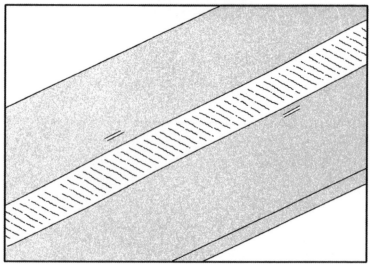

fiction

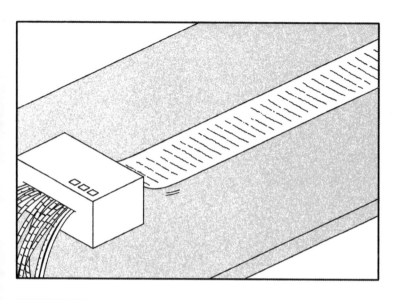

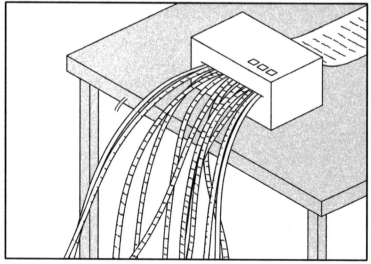

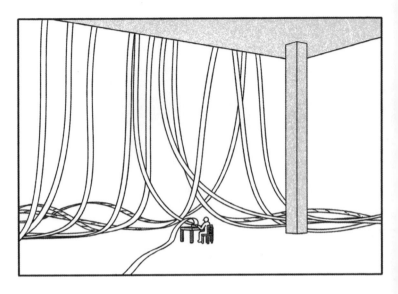

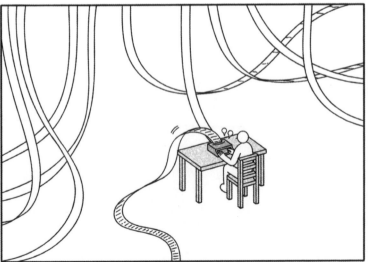

fiction

20km/h

20km /h

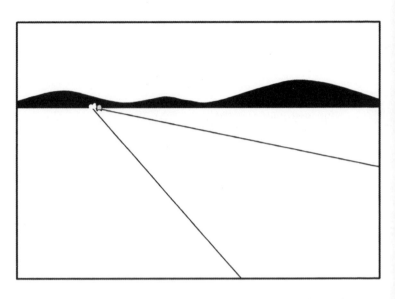

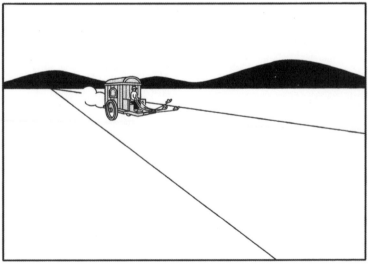

20km/h

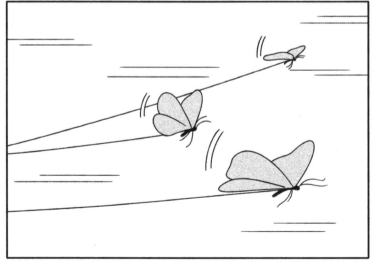

20km/h

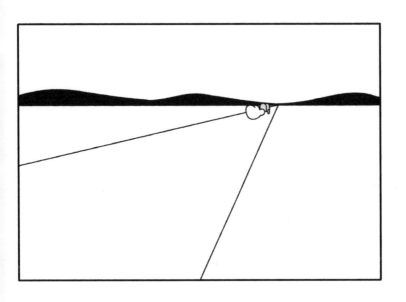

air bubble

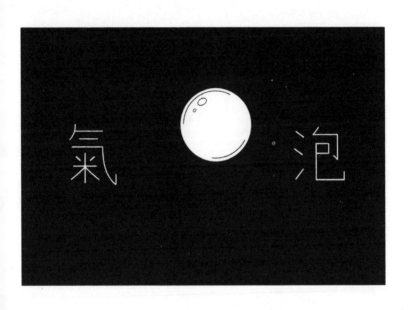

氣　〇　泡

air bubble

氣泡

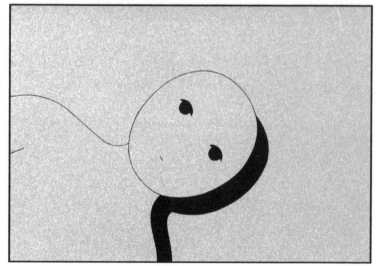

air bubble

balcony

陽　　　　　台

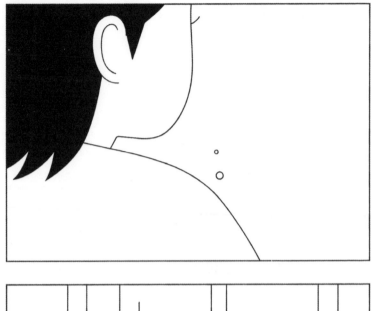

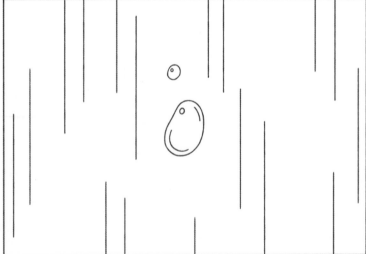

balcony

balcony

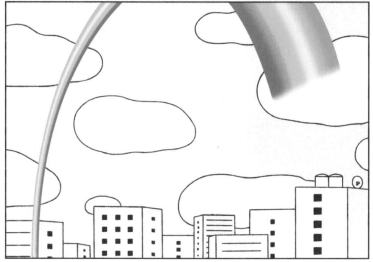

balcony

hotel

旅 ⊝— 店

hotel

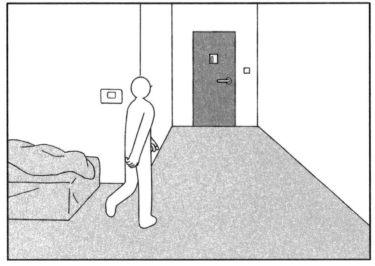

旅店

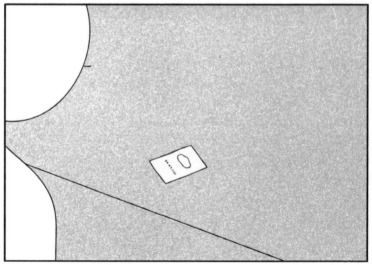

hotel

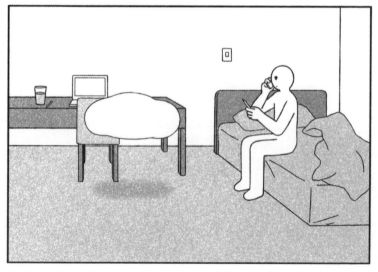

hotel

旅店

seed

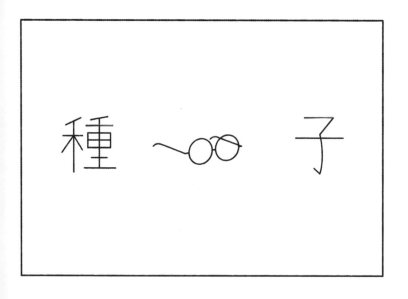

種 ～∞ 子

seed

種子

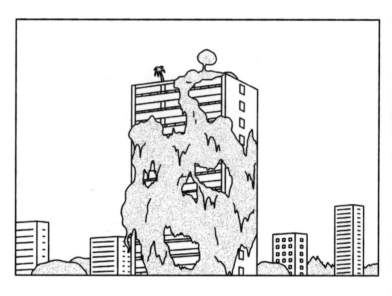

seed

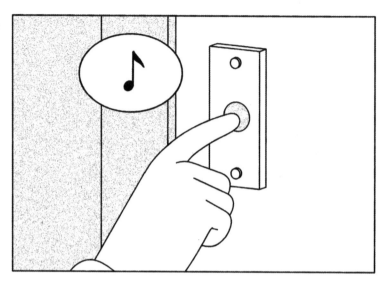

種子

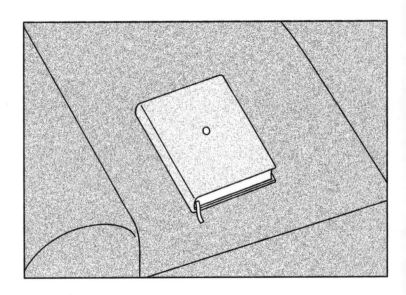

seed

hole

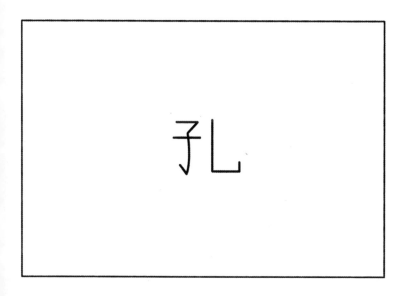

孔

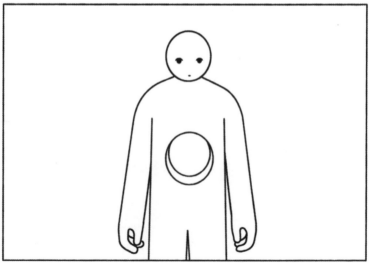

hole

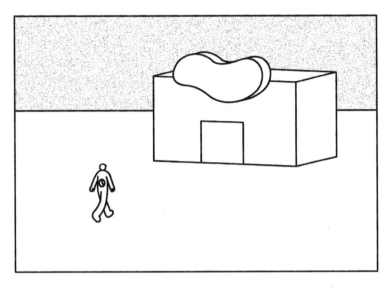

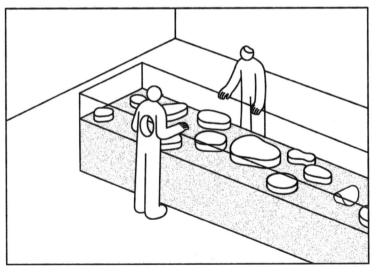

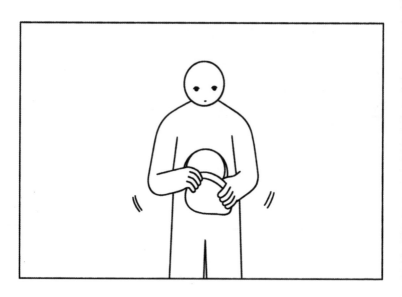

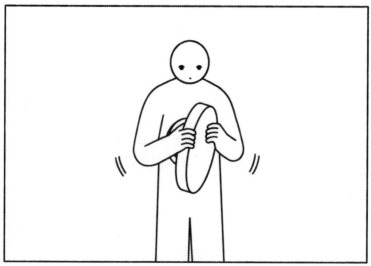

hole

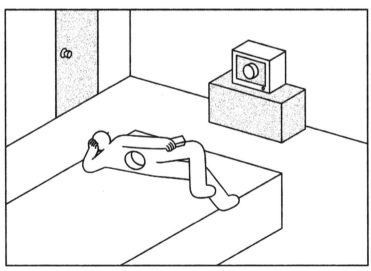

sort

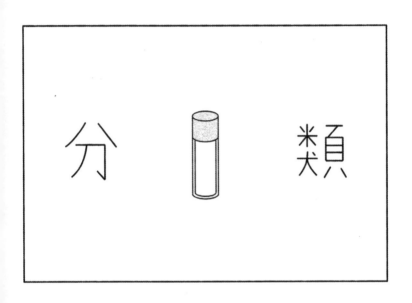

分　🧪　類

sort

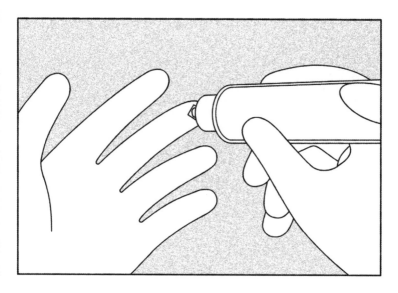

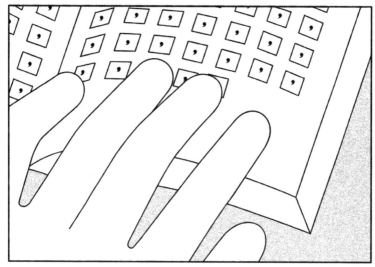

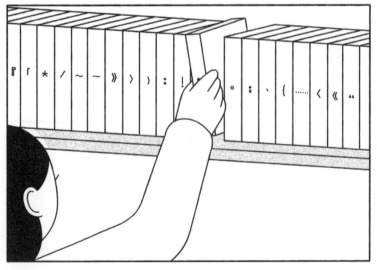

sort

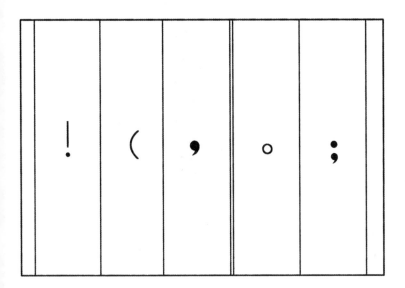

key

鑰 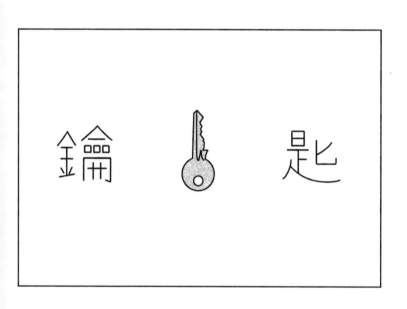 匙

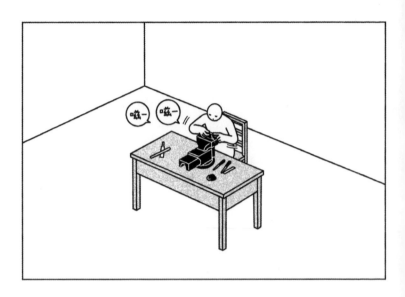

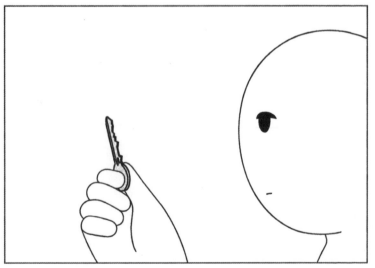

key

鑰匙

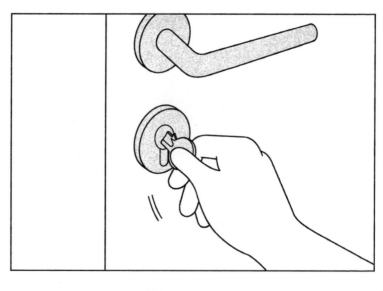

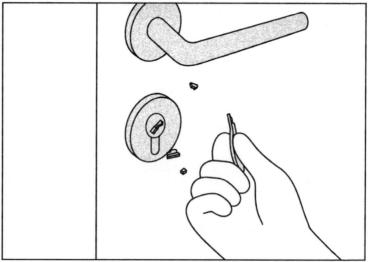

key

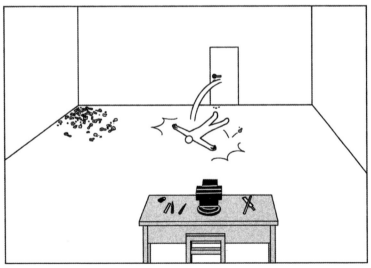

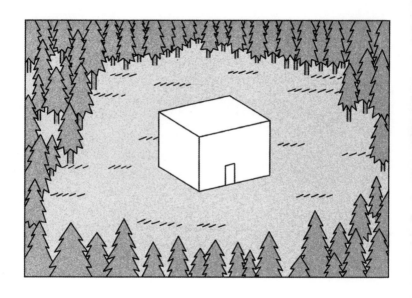

key

ZOO

動　物　園

ZOO

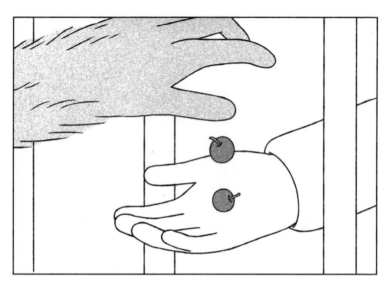

動物園

cave

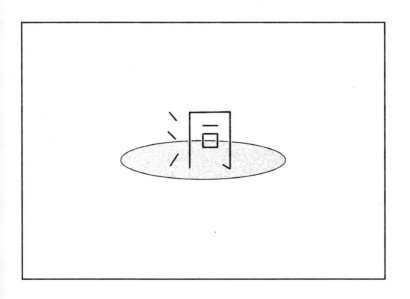

cave

洞

cave

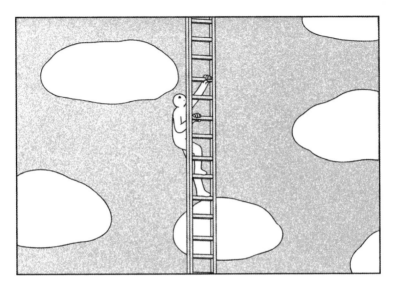

洞

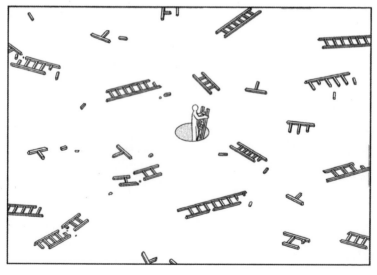

cave

洞

mirror

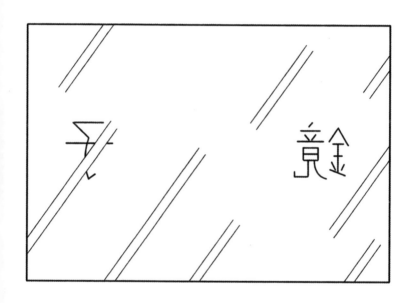

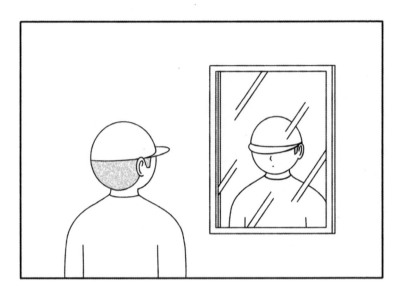

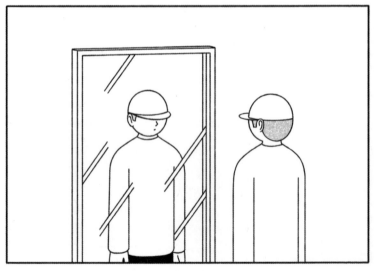

mirror

鏡子

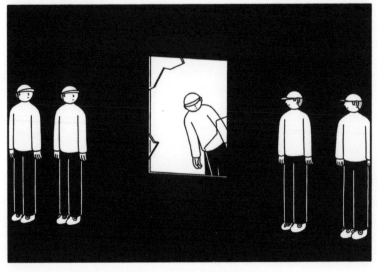

mirror

oversleep

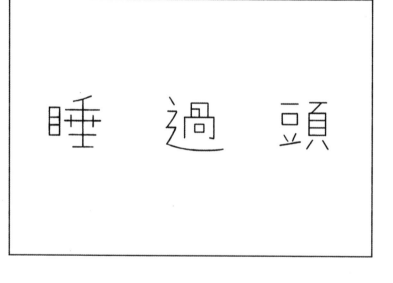

睡　過　頭

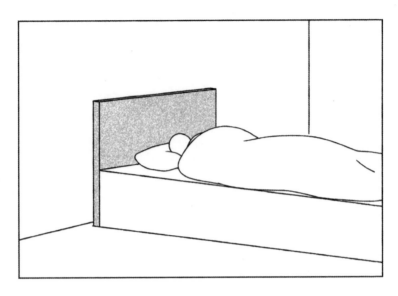

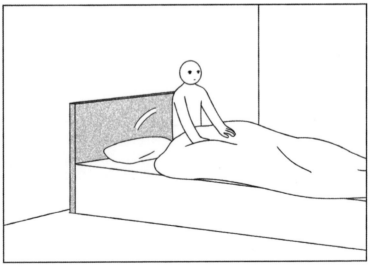

oversleep

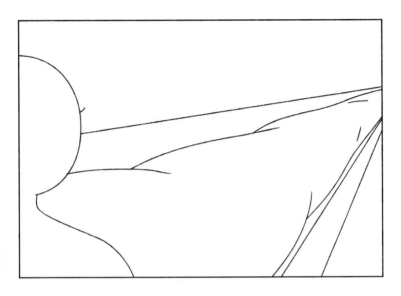

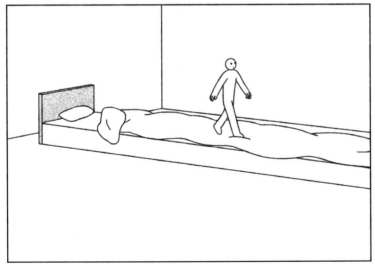

睡過頭

oversleep

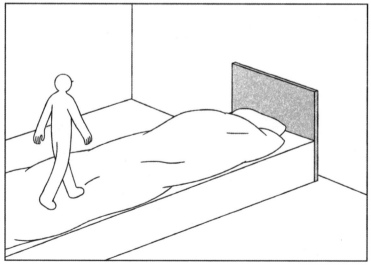

睡過頭

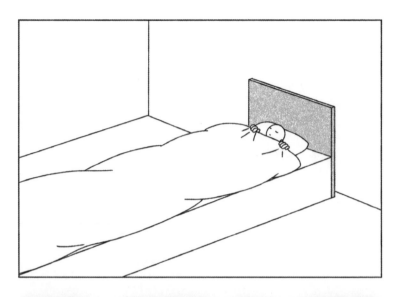

oversleep

earth

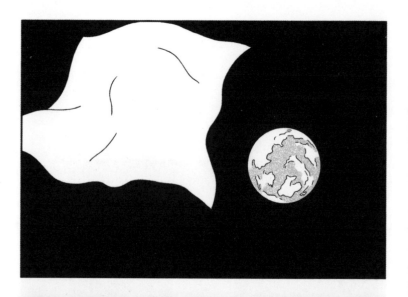

earth

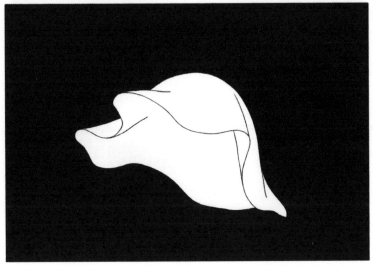

earth

地球

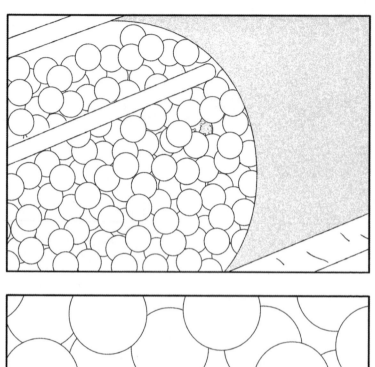

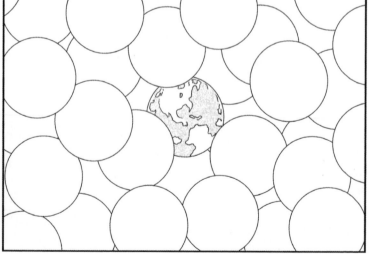

earth

part time

兼 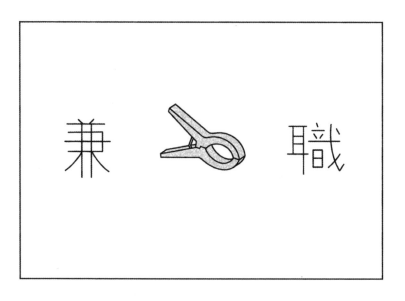 職

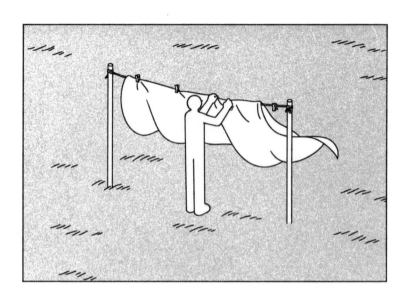

part time

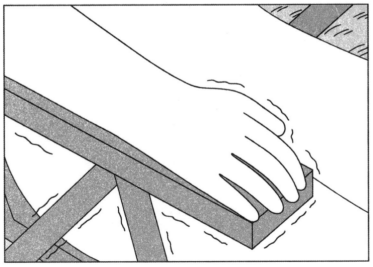

part time

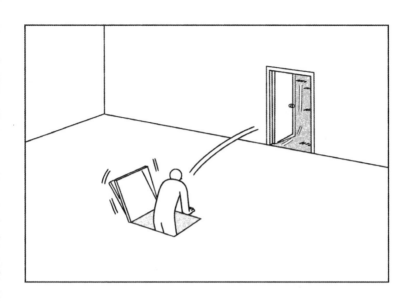

兼職

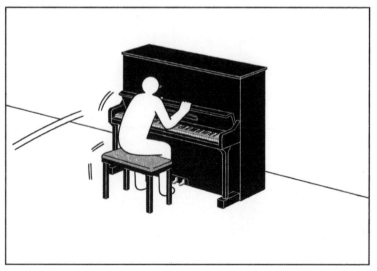

part time

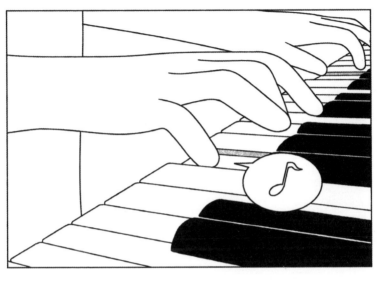

part time

兼職

appointment

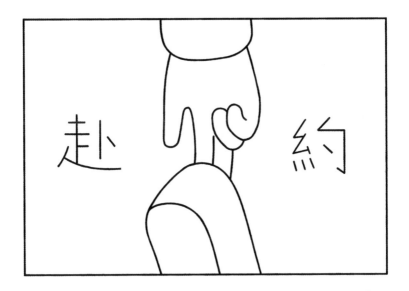

赴約

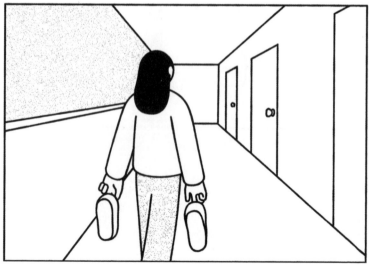

appointment

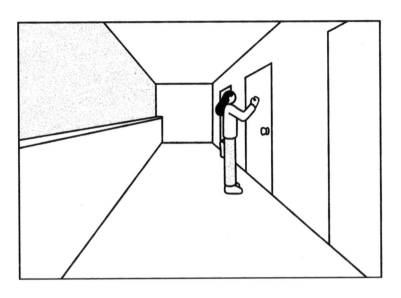

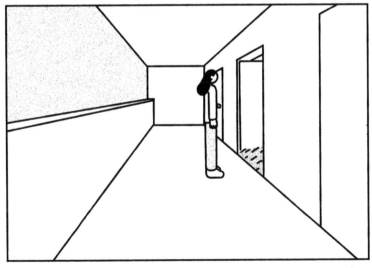

赴約

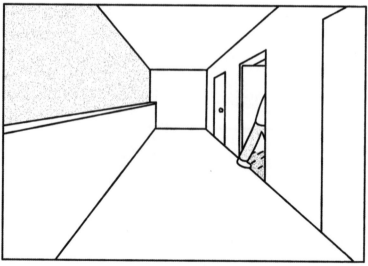

appointment

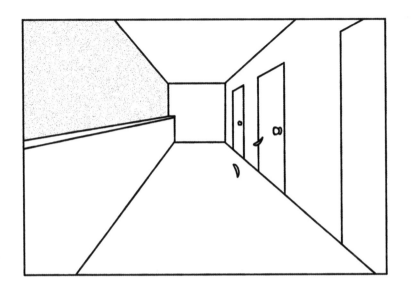

赴約

puzzle

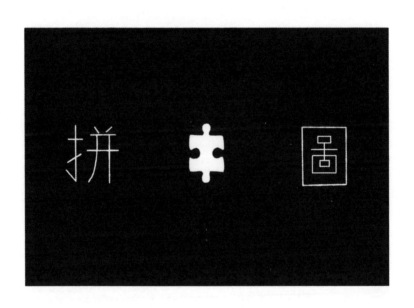

puzzle

拼圖

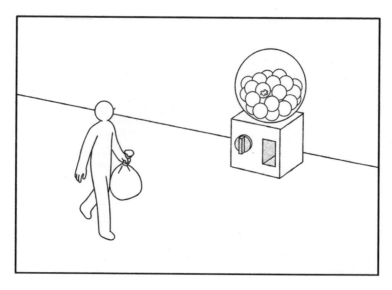

puzzle

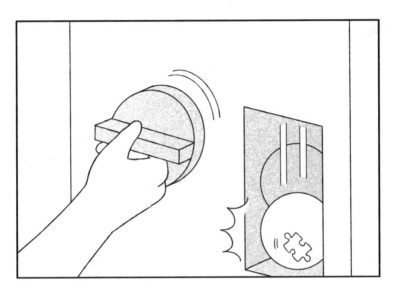

拼圖

puzzle

拼圖

puzzle

拼圖

puzzle

sleep

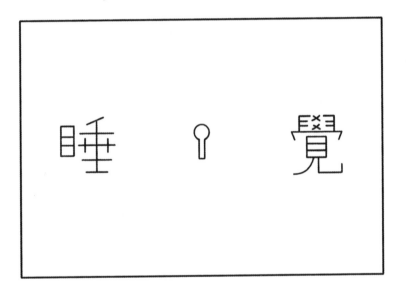

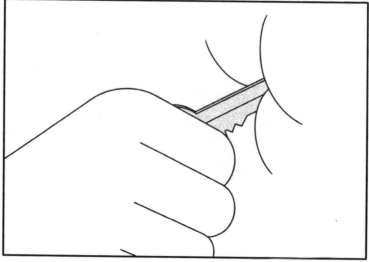

sleep

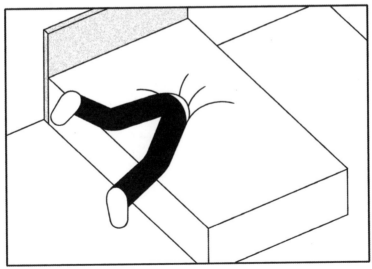

睡覺

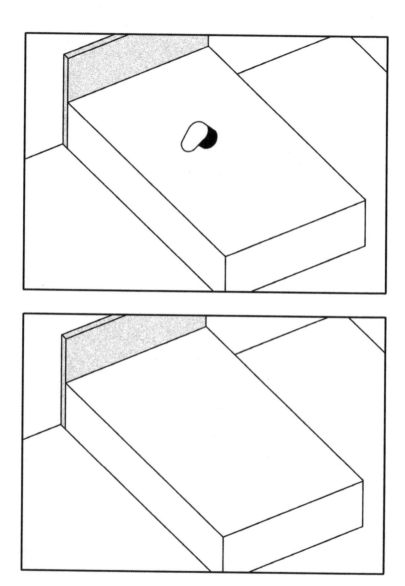

sleep

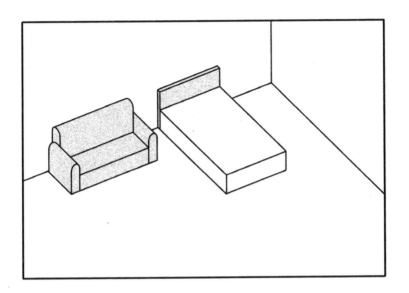

night

夜　　晚

night

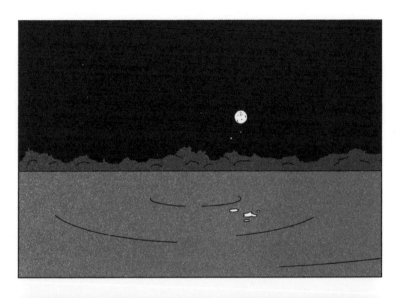

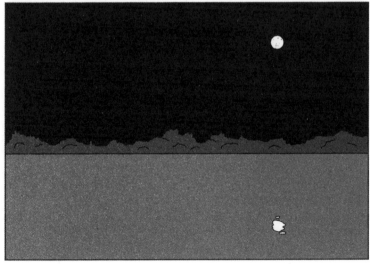

夜晚

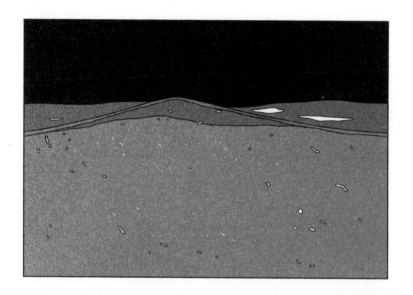

night

夜晚

game

遊 戲

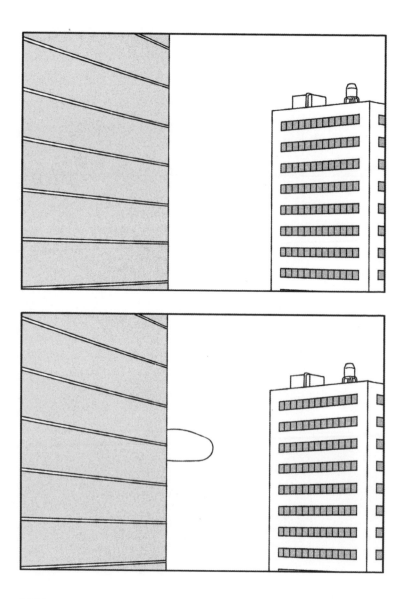

game

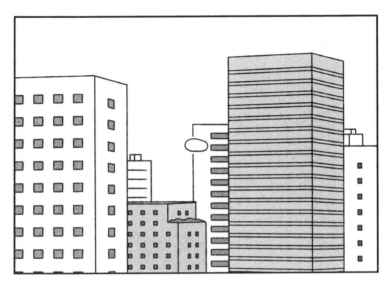

遊戲

game

遊戲

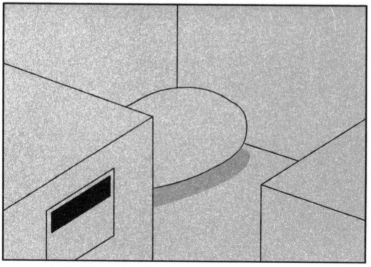

game

遊戲

WANDER 002

20KM/H

● 作者 —— 我是白 WOSHIBAI ● 設計 —— 鄧彧 tengyulab.com ● 社長暨總編輯 —— 湯皓全

● 出版 —— 鯨嶼文化有限公司 ● 地址 —— 231 新北市新店區民權路 108-3 號 6 樓

● 電話 —— (02) 22181417 ● 傳真 —— (02) 86672166

● 讀書共和國集團社長 —— 郭重興 ● 發行人暨出版總監 —— 曾大福

● 發行 —— 遠足文化事業股份有限公司 ● 地址 —— 231 新北市新店區民權路 108-3 號 8 樓

● 電話 —— (02) 22181417 ● 傳真 —— (02) 86671065 ● 電子信箱 —— service@bookrep.com.tw

● 客服專線 —— 0800-221-029 ● 法律顧問 —— 華洋國際專利事務所 蘇文生律師

● 印刷 —— 和楹印刷有限公司 ● 初版 —— 2022 年 6 月 ● 定價 —— 580 元

WOSHIBAI